多才多藝的格麗施

作者：瑪麗‧霍夫曼
插圖：卡羅琳‧賓奇

For Buchi Emecheta *M.H.*
For Joe *C.B.*

Amazing Grace

Written by
Mary Hoffman

Illustrated by
Caroline Binch

Translated by East Word

Magi Publications, London

格麗施是一個特別喜愛故事的女孩。

不論是讀給她聽、講給她聽或她自己編造的......。也不管這些故事是書上的、電視上的、電影裡的或錄影帶上的,或是出自婆婆那久遠的記憶中的。格麗施就是喜愛故事。

她在聽完了故事之後,或在故事正講了一半時,格麗施就會扮演故事的角色。最精彩的角色總是由她扮演。

Grace was a girl who loved stories.
She didn't mind if they were read to her or told to her or made up in her own head. She didn't care if they were from books or on TV or in films or on the video or out of Nana's long memory. Grace just loved stories.
And after she had heard them, or sometimes while they were still going on, Grace would act them out. And she always gave herself the most exciting part.

格麗施扮做聖女貞德去參加戰鬥......

Grace went into battle as Joan of Arc . . .

裝作蜘蛛人編織一張邪惡的蜘蛛網。

and wove a wicked web as Anansi the spiderman.

她躲藏在特洛伊城門的木馬中......

She hid inside the wooden horse at the gates of Troy . . .

她隨漢尼拔和一百頭大象跨過阿爾卑斯山......

she crossed the Alps with Hannibal and a hundred elephants . . .

她拖著一條假腿、
帶著一隻鸚鵡橫渡七海。

**she sailed the seven seas with a peg-leg
and a parrot.**

她是印第安酋長，坐在波光粼粼的大湖邊，

She was Hiawatha, sitting by the shining Big-Sea-Water

還在後花園的森林中扮做狼孩。

and Mowgli in the back garden jungle.

但格麗施最喜愛的是表演鬧劇。她喜歡扮做惠廷頓轉身聆聽倫敦城鐘聲的召喚；或扮做擦拭神燈的阿拉丁。鬧劇中最出色的人物都是男孩子，但格麗施也照學不誤。

But most of all Grace loved to act pantomimes. She liked to be Dick Whittington turning to hear the bells of London Town or Aladdin rubbing the magic lamp. The best characters in pantomimes were boys, but Grace played them anyway.

在周圍沒有人的時候，格麗施一個人扮演所有的角色。她成了一個上千人的劇組。小貓"波波"通常也助一臂之力。

如果媽媽和婆婆不太忙，她也能勸說她們加入。那時，她就成了格麗施醫生，媽媽和婆婆的生命就要任她擺布了！

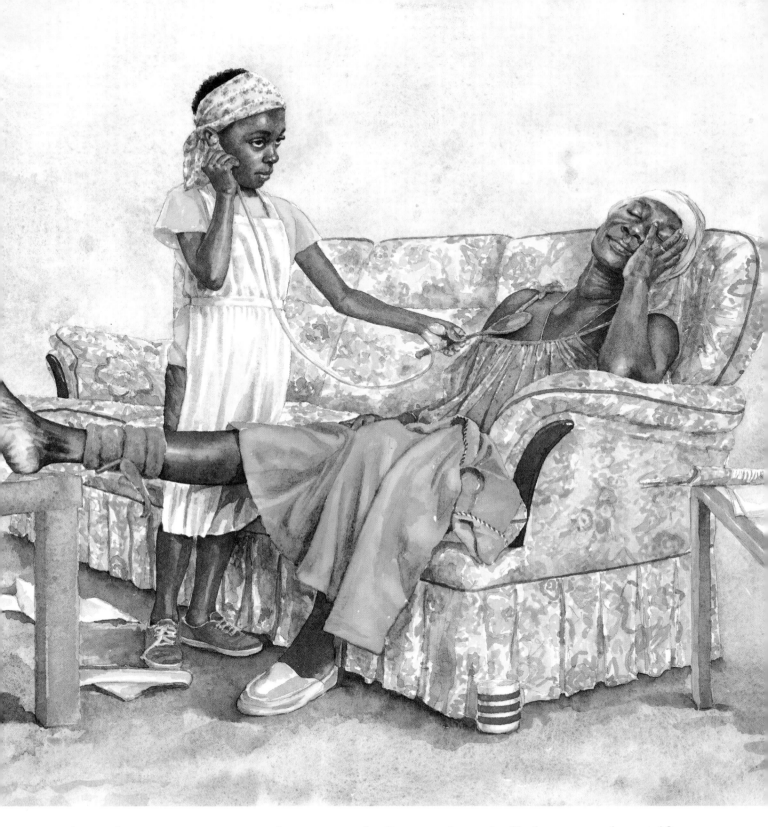

When there was no-one else around, Grace played all the parts herself.
She was a cast of thousands. Paw-Paw the cat usually helped out.
And sometimes she could persuade Ma and Nana to join in, when they
weren't too busy. Then she was Doctor Grace and their lives were in
her hands.

一天在學校，格麗施的老師說他們要演"潘彼得"一劇。格麗施舉起手要
演......潘彼得。

"你不能叫彼得，"拉杰說。"那是一個男孩子的名字。"但格麗施的手還是舉著。

"你不能演潘彼得，"納坦莉悄聲說。"他不是黑人。"但格麗施的手還是舉著。

"好了，"老師說。"你們許多人都想扮演潘彼得，所以我們得進行試演。
我們下星期一選角色。"

One day at school her teacher said they were going to do the play of *Peter Pan*. Grace put up her hand to be . . . Peter Pan.

"You can't be called Peter," said Raj. "That's a boy's name."

But Grace kept her hand up.

"You can't be Peter Pan," whispered Natalie. "He wasn't black."

But Grace kept her hand up.

"All right," said the teacher. "Lots of you want to be Peter Pan, so we'll have to have auditions. We'll choose the parts next Monday."

格麗施回到家裡，看上去挺難過的。

"怎麼啦?" 媽媽問。

"拉杰說，因爲我是女孩子，所以我不能演潘彼得。

"這表明拉杰根本不懂，" 媽說。"潘彼得總
是女孩子扮演的!"

When Grace got home, she seemed
rather sad.
''What's the matter?'' asked Ma.
''Raj said I couldn't be Peter Pan because
I'm a girl.''
''That just shows all Raj knows about it,''
said Ma. ''Peter Pan is *always* a girl!''

格麗施高興了起來，後來她又想起了另一件事。 "納坦莉說我不能扮
潘彼得，因爲我是黑人，" 她說。媽有些生氣，但婆婆制止了她。
"看來納坦莉又是一個一無所知的人，" 她說。 "如果你用心，
你可以成爲任何人物。"

Grace cheered up, then later she remembered something else.
"Natalie says I can't be Peter Pan because I'm black," she said.
Ma started to get angry but Nana stopped her.
"It seems that Natalie is another one who don't know nothing," she
said. "You can be anything you want, Grace, if you put your mind to it."

第二天是星期六，婆婆對格麗施說她們要出門。
下午，她們搭巴士和火車進了城。婆婆帶格麗施來到一家大劇院前。外面的招牌上以光彩奪目的霓虹燈寫著"羅薩麗•威爾金斯主演《羅密歐與朱麗葉》"。

Next day was Saturday and Nana told Grace they were going out.
In the afternoon they caught a bus and a train into town.
Nana took Grace to a grand theatre. Outside it said,
"ROSALIE WILKINS in ROMEO AND JULIET" in beautiful sparkling lights.

"我們是去看芭蕾嗎，婆婆?" 格麗施問。

"是的，親愛的，可是我要你先看看這些廣告畫。"

婆婆指給格麗施看一些照片，上面有一個美麗的女孩穿著芭蕾舞短裙舞。

其中一幅照片上寫著: "新朱麗葉，一枝獨秀"。

'Are we going to the ballet, Nana?'' asked Grace.
"We are, Honey, but I want you to look at these pictures first.''
Nana showed Grace some photographs of a beautiful young girl dancer
in a tutu. ''STUNNING NEW JULIET!'' it said on one of them.

　　"照片上的那個是家鄉千里達的小羅薩麗，" 婆婆說。 "她的婆婆和我從小是一起在島上長大的。她總是問我是不是要票看她的小孫女跳舞 - 所以，這次我說是。"

"That one is little Rosalie from back home in Trinidad,"
said Nana. "Her Granny and me, we grew up together on the island.
She's always asking me do I want tickets to see her little girl dance –
so this time I said yes."

看完芭蕾，格麗斯扮演起朱麗葉的角色，穿著她想像中的芭蕾舞短裙在她的房間裡翩翩起舞。 "我扮什麼人都可以，" 她想道。 "我還可以 扮潘彼得。"

After the ballet, Grace played the part of Juliet, dancing around her room in her imaginary tutu. "I can be anything I want," she thought. "I can even be Peter Pan."

星期一那天，進行了試演。老師讓全班人對角色進行表決。拉杰被挑選扮演 "鐵鈎" 船長。納坦莉演溫迪。

然後他們開始挑選潘彼得。

格麗施對動做、言詞完全有把握。那個角色她在家裡經常扮演。所有的小朋友都投了她的票。

"你太出色了，" 納坦莉説。

On Monday they had the auditions. Their teacher let the class vote on the parts. Raj was chosen to play Captain Hook. Natalie was going to be Wendy. Then they had to choose Peter Pan.
Grace knew exactly what to do – and all the words to say. It was a part she had often played at home. All the children voted for her.
''You were great,'' said Natalie.

演出極爲成功，格麗施扮演的潘彼得真令人贊嘆。

演出結束後，她說：“我覺得我可以一路飛回家了！”

“這有可能，”她說。

“是啊，”婆婆說。“如果格麗施用心的話－她想做什麼都可以。”

The play was a great success and Grace was an amazing Peter Pan.
After it was all over, she said, ''I feel as if I could fly all the way home!''
''You probably could,'' said Ma.
''Yes,'' said Nana. ''If Grace put her mind to it – she can do anything
she want.''